Mel Bay Presents

Scottish Songbook for
Hammered Dulcimer

by Jeanne Page

1 2 3 4 5 6 7 8 9 0

Visit us on the Web at www.melbay.com — E-mail us at email@melbay.com

TABLE OF CONTENTS

ABOUT THE AUTHOR

Jeanne Page began her life-long journey into folk music at age 12, singing and playing the guitar. Since then, she has gravitated to focus primarily on the hammered dulcimer and celtic harp. She teaches both instruments privately and through the University of New Mexico. Jeanne is the Director of a youth harp ensemble called the "Apple Mountain Harp Kids," and co-founded with her husband, Shane, the Apple Mountain Dulcimer Club and the Apple Mountain Harp Circle. She also directs the "Harps in Healing Service Program" in Albuquerque, New Mexico. Jeanne has been performing solo and with the Celtic/Folk band "Heirlooms" since 1992, and has several instructional books available through Mel Bay Publications including *Hammered Dulcimer Chords* (MB96675), *Arranging for Hammered Dulcimer*, and *Hammered Dulcimer 2000*.

BEFORE YOU BEGIN...

This collection includes the following for each song:

• A "melody only" version.
• An intermediate arranged version.
• Words (where applicable).
• Guitar chords.

The melody version can be used in the following ways:

• As a beginning level version.
• As a tool for intermediate players. It is best to practice just the melody and know it well before you begin the arranged version. This better equips you to emphasize the melody and to keep it from being buried in a complicated arrangement.
• When performing a tune, play the "melody only" version the first time through and then the arranged version the second time through.
• As a lead line for other instruments such as fiddle or penny whistle, when playing in an ensemble.
• In a dulcimer club setting, the beginners can play this version, while intermediates play the other.

The arranged version can be used in the following ways:

• As a "stand alone" arrangement.
• As a starting place for advanced players who may choose to add more arpeggios, fills, scale runs, etc.
• In a dulcimer club setting, the intermediate players can play this version while the beginners play the melody only.

The chords are noted above the staff to be used in the following ways:

• For chordal backup on the hammered dulcimer while singing.
• For chordal backup on the hammered dulcimer while other instruments play the lead in an ensemble.
• For other instruments, such as guitar, to play backup for the hammered dulcimer lead.

The words are included so you can also sing these songs with your instrument.

ABOUT TABLATURE...

Tablature systems have been created to make a new instrument more accessible to the musician. While many TAB systems accomplish this smoothly and effectively (the mountain dulcimer is a great example), I have yet to see a hammered dulcimer version that wasn't at least as time consuming to learn as standard musical notation. Often it is more challenging! Until some wise and creative person comes up with a system that simplifies the process of learning music on the hammered dulcimer, I will continue to recommend that players learn standard musical notation on the treble staff.

The graph here is intended to help you accomplish this task and to locate the notes you are searching for in the written music. Keep it right next to you when working a song so that you can refer to it often. There are also some wonderful introductory books for hammered dulcimer that explain the logic of the instrument, where different keys are located, etc., which will make the process easier to manage.

Have fun with these tunes–I hope you enjoy them as much as I do!

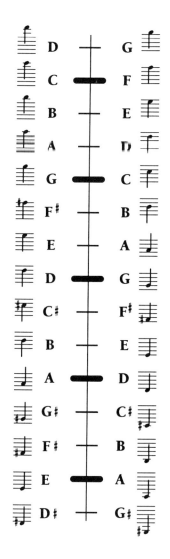
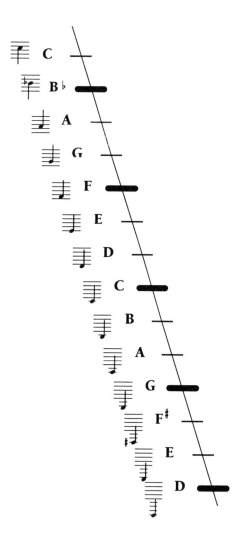

A FEW NOTES...

The following tunes are credited to Scottish poet and composer, Robert Burns:

Auld Lang Syne
Comin' Through the Rye
Flow Gently Sweet Afton
John Anderson, My Jo
My Heart's in the Highlands
O Whistle and I'll Come to Ye Me Lad
Scots Wha Hae
Will Ye No Come Back Again?

The Bluebells of Scotland is credited to Mrs. Jordan
Jock O' Hazeldean is credited to Sir Walter Scott (lyrics)
Skye Boat Song is credited to Harold Boulton (lyrics)

To the best of my knowledge, all others are traditional, the composer and/or author unknown.

THE SONGS

SCOTTISH SONGBOOK FOR HAMMERED DULCIMER

Annie Laurie

1. Maxwelton's braes are bonnie, where early fa's the dew,
And it's there that Annie Laurie gave me her promise true.
Gave me her promise true, which ne'er forgot will be,
And for bonnie Annie Laurie, I'd lay me doon and dee.

2. Her brow is like the snawdrift, her neck is like the swan,
Her face it is the fairest that e'er the sun shone on.
That e'er the sun shone on, and dark blue is her e'e,
And for bonnie Annie Laurie, I'd lay me doon and dee.

Annie Laurie

3. Like dew on the gowan lying, is the fa' o' her fairy feet,
And like winds in summer sighing, her voice is low and sweet.
Her voice is low and sweet, and she's the world to me,
And for bonnie Annie Laurie, I'd lay me doon and dee.

Arran Boat Song

Arran Boat Song

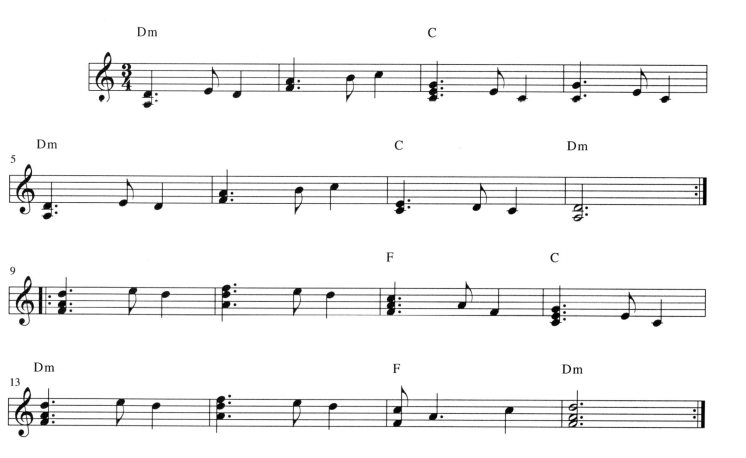

Auld Lang Syne

1. Should auld acquaintance be forgot and never brought to mind?
Should auld acquaintance be forgot, and days o' lang syne.

Chorus:
For auld land syne, my dear, for auld lang syne,
We'll take a cup o' kindness yet for auld lang syne.

Auld Lang Syne

2. And surely ye'll be your pintstowp, and surely I'll be mine,
And we'll take a cup o' kindness yet for auld lang syne.

3. We twa hae run about the braes and pou'd the gowans fine,
But we've wandered mony a weary foot sin auld lang syne.

The Blue Bells of Scotland

1. Oh where, tell me where is your Highland laddie gone?
Oh where, tell me where is your Highland laddie gone?
He's gone with streaming banners where noble deeds are done.
And it's oh, in my heart I wish him safe at home.

2. Oh where, tell me where did your Highland laddie dwell?
Oh where, tell me where did your Highland laddie dwell?
He dwelt in bonnie Scotland, where blooms the sweet blue bell
And it's oh, in my heart I loved my laddie well.

The Blue Bells of Scotland

3. Oh what, tell me what does your Highland laddie wear?
Oh what, tell me what does your Highland laddie wear?
A bonnet with a lofty plume, and on his breast a plaid,
And it's oh, in my heart I love my Highland lad.

Bonnie Dundee

1. To the Lords of Convention 'twas Claverhouse spoke,
Ere the King's crown go down there are crowns to be broke,
So each cavalier who loves honor and me,
Let him follow the bonnets of Bonnie Dundee.

Chorus:
Come fill up my cup, come fill up my can,
Come saddle my horses, and call out my men,
Unhook the West Port and let us go free,
For it's up with the bonnets of Bonnie Dundee.

Bonnie Dundee

2. Dundee he is mounted, he rides up the street,
The bells they ring backward, the drums they are beat,
But the provost said: "Just e'en let it be,
For the town is weel rid o' that devil o' Dundee."

3. There are hills beyond Pentland, and lands beyond Forth
Be there lords of the south, there are chiefs in the north,
There are brave Duinnewassals, three thousand times three,
Will cry, "Hey, for the bonnets of Bonnie Dundee."

Comin' Thro' the Rye

1. Gin' a body meet a body, comin' thro' the rye,
Gin' a body kiss a body, need a body cry?
Ilka lassie has her laddie, nane they say ha'e I,
Yet all the lads they smile at me, when comin' thro' the rye.

2. Gin' a body meet a body, comin' frae the well,
Gin' a body kiss a body, need a body tell?
Ilka lassie has her laddie, ne'er a ane ha'e I
But all the lads they smile on me when comin' thro' the rye.

Comin' Thro' the Rye

3. Gin' a body meet a body comin' frae the town,
Gin' a body greet a body need a body frown?
Ilka lassie has her laddie, nane they say ha'e I
But all the lads they love me well, and what the waur am I

4. Amang the train there is a swain I dearly love myself
But whaur his hame, or what his name, I dinna care to tell
Ilka lassie has her laddie, nane they say ha'e I
But all the lads they love me well, and what the waur am I

Farewell to Tarwathie

1. Farewell to Tarwathie, adieu Mormond Hill,
And the dear land of Crimmond, I bid you farewell
I am bound now for Greenland and ready to sail,
In hopes to find riches in hunting the whale.

2. Our ship is well rigged and ready to sail
Our crew they are anxious to follow the whale,
Where the icebergs do float and the stormy winds blow,
And the land and the ocean are covered with snow.

Farewell to Tarwathie

3. The cold coast of Greenland is barren and bare,
No seedtime or harvest is ever known there,
And the birds here sing sweetly on mountain and dale,
But there isna a birdie to sing to the whale.

Flow Gently, Sweet Afton

Lyrics on page 62.

Flow Gently, Sweet Afton

Lyrics on page 62.

The Four Marys

Chorus: Last night there were four Marys, tonight there'll be but three
There was Mary Seaton, and Mary Beaton, and Mary Carmichael and me.

1. Oh, often have I dressed my queen and put on her braw silk gown
But all the thanks I've got tonight, is to be hanged in Edinborough town.

2. Full often have I dressed my queen, put gold upon her hair
But I have got for my reward, the gallows to be my share.

The Four Marys

3. Oh little did my mother know, the day she cradled me
The land I was to travel in, the death I was to dee.

4. O happy, happy is the maid that's born of beauty free,
Oh it was my rosy dimpled cheeks that's been the devil to me.

5. They'll tie a kerchief around my eyes, that I may not see to dee,
And they'll never tell my father or mother but that I'm across the sea.

The Great Silkie

1. "An earthly nouris sits and sings and aye, she sings be lilly wean
Little ken I my Bairny's father far less the land that he staps in."

2. Then in steps he to her bed fit, and a grumley guest I'm sure was he,
Saying, "Here I am, thy bairny's father, although I be not comely."

3. "I am a man upon the land, and I am a silkie in the sea
And when I'm far and far from land, my home it is in Skule Skerry."

4. "It was na' weel," quo' the maiden fair, "It was na' weel," indeed quo' she.
"That the great silkie from Sule Skerry, should hae come and brought a bairn to me."

The Great Silkie

5. Then he has taken a purse of gold, and he has pat it upon her knee,
Saying, "Gie to me my little young son, and take thee up thy nourris fee."

6. "And it shall come to pass on a simmer's day, when the sun shines het on ev'ra stane,
That I shall take my little young son, and teach him for tae swim the faem."

7. "And thou shall marry a proud gunner, and a richt guid gunner I'm sure he'll be,
But the vera first shot that ere he'll shoot, He'll kill baith my young son and me."

8. "Alas, alas," the maiden cried, "This weary fate that's laid on me"
And once she sobbed and once she sighed, and her tender heart did break in three.

Jock O' Hazeldean

Lyrics on page 63.

Jock O' Hazeldean

Lyrics on page 63.

John Anderson My Jo

1. John Anderson my Jo, John, when we were first acquent
Your locks were like the raven, your bonnie brow was bent
But now your brow is beld, John your locks are like the snaw
But blessings on your frosty pow, John Anderson, my Jo.

John Anderson My Jo

2. John Anderson, my Jo, we clamb the hill together,
And mony a canty day, John, we've had wi' ane anither,
Now we maun totter down, John, but hand in hand we'll go,
And we'll sleep together at the foot, John Anderson, my Jo.

Johnny Cope

1. Cope sent a challenge frae Dunbar saying, Charlie meet me an' ye daur
And I'll learn you the art of war if ye'll meet wi' me in the morning.

Chorus:
Hey! Johnny Cope are ye waulkin' yet? Or are your drums a-beatin' yet,
If ye were waulking' I had wait to gang tae the coals in the morning.

2. When Charlie looked the letter upon, he drew his sword the scabbard from
"Come follow me my merry men, and we'll meet Johnny Cope in the morning."

Johnny Cope

3. "Now Johnny, be as guid's your word, come let us try faith fire and sword;
And dinna run awa' like a frightened bird, that's chased frae its nest in the morning."

Lassie with the Yellow Coatie

1. Lassie with the yellow coatie, will ye wed an muirlan' jockie?
Lassie with the yellow coatie, will ye busk and gang with me?

2. I hae meal and milk a plenty, I hae kail and cakes fu' dainty,
I've a but an' ben fu' genty, but I want a wife like thee

3. Although my mailen be but sma', An' little gowd I hae to shaw
I hae a heart without a flaw, an' I will gie it a' to thee.

Lassie with the Yellow Coatie

4. Wi' my lassie an' my doggie, o'er the lea an' through the boggie,
Nane on earth was e'er sae vogie, or as blythe as we will be.

5. Haste ye, lassie, to my bosom, while the roses are in blossom,
Time is precious, dinna lose them flowers will fade, an' sae will ye

6. Lassie wi' the yellow coatie, ah! tak' pity on your Jockie,
Lassie wi' the yellow coatie, I'm in haste, an' sae should ye

29

Loch Lomond

1. By yon bonnie banks and by yon bonnie braes, where the sun shines bright on Loch Lomond
Where me and my true love were ever wont to gae, on the bonnie, bonnie banks of Loch Lomond

Chorus:
O, ye'll take the high road and I'll take the low road, and I'll be in Scotland afore ye
But me and my true love will never meet again, on the bonnie, bonnie banks of Loch Lomond

Loch Lomond

2. 'Twas there where we parted in yon shady glen, on the steep, steep side o' Ben Lomond,
Where in purple hue the Hieland hills we view, and the moon comin' out in the gloamin'

3. The wee birdies sing and the wild flowers spring, and in sunshine the waters are sleepin'
But the broken heart it kens, nae second spring, tho' the waefu' may cease frae their greetin'

MacPherson's Farewell

1. Farewell, ye dungeions dark and strong, the wretch's destiny
MacPherson's time will not be long on yonder gallows tree.

Chorus:
Sae rantingly, sae wantonly, sae dauntingly gaed he,
He played a tune and danced it round below the gallows tree

2. O, what is death but parting breath? On many a bloody plain
I've dared his face, and in this place I scorn him yet again

MacPherson's Farewell

3. Untie these bands from off my hands, and bring to me my sword
And there's no a man in all Scotland, but I'll brave him at a word

4. I've lived a life of sturt and strife, I die by treachery
It burns my heart I must depart, and not avenged be

5. Now farewell light, thou sunshine bright, and all beneath the sky
May coward shame distain his name the wretch that dare not die

Maids When You're Young

Lyrics on page 64.

Maids When You're Young

Lyrics on page 64.

Mairi's Wedding

Chorus:
Step we gladly on we go, heel for heel and toe for toe
Arm and arm and row on row all for Mairi's wedding.

1. Over hillways up and down, myrtle green and bracken brown
Past the sheiling, through the town, all for the sake of Mairi

Mairi's Wedding

2. Red her cheeks as rowans are, bright her eye as any star,
Fairest of them all by far, that's our darling Mairi

3. Plenty herring, plenty meal, plenty peat to fill her creel,
Plenty bonnie bairns as well, that's the toast for Mairi

Mist Covered Mountains of Home

Mist Covered Mountains of Home

My Heart's in the Highlands

1. My heart's in the highlands, my heart is not here,
My heart's in the highlands a chasing the deer
A chasing the wild deer, and following the roe
My heart's in the highlands, wherever I go

2. Farewell to the Highlands, farewell to the North
The birthplace of valour, the country of worth
Wherever I wander, wherever I rove
The hills of the highlands for ever I love

My Heart's in the Highlands

3. Farewell to the mountains high covered with snow
Farewell to the straths and green valleys below
Farewell to the forests and wild-hanging woods
Farewell to the torrents and loud-pouring floods

O Whistle and I'll Come to Ye Me Lad

Chorus:
O, whistle and I'll come to ye, me lad
O, whistle and I'll come to ye, me lad
Though father and mother and all should go mad
O, whistle and I'll come to ye, me lad

1. But warily tent when ye come to court me
And come nae unless the back yett be a jee
Syne up the back style, and let nobody see
And come as ye were na comin to me

O Whistle and I'll Come to Ye Me Lad

2. At kirk, or at market, whenever you meet me
Gang by me as though that ye cared not a flie
But steal me a blink of your bonnie black e'e
Yet look as ye were na lookin to me

3. Ay vow and protest that ye care na for me
And whyles ye may lightly my beauty a wee
But court na anither though jokin' ye be
For fear that she wyle your fancy frae me

Scotland the Brave

Scotland the Brave

Scots Wha Hae

1. Scots wha hae wi' Wallace bled, Scots wham Bruce has aften led
Welcome to your gory bed, or to victory
Now's the day, and now's the hour, see the front of battle lour,
See approach proud Edward's power, chains and slavery

2. Wha will be a traitor knave? Wha can fill a coward's grave?
Wha sae base as be a slave? Let him turn and flee
Wha for Scotland's King and law, freedom's sword will strongly draw
Freeman stand or freeman fa', let him on wi' me

Scots Wha Hae

3. By Oppression's woes and pains, by your sons in servile chains
We will drain our dearest veins but they shall be free
Lay the proud usurpers low, tyrants fall in every foe
Liberty's in every blow, let us do, or dee.

The Shearin's No For You

Oh the shearin's no for you my bonnie lassie oh
Oh the shearin's no for you my bonnie lassie oh
Oh the shearin's no for you
For your back it winna bou
And your belly's rowrin' fu' my bonnie lassie oh

The Shearin's No For You

Skye Boat Song

Chorus:
Speed bonnie boat like a bird on a wing, onward the sailors cry
Carry the lad that's born to be King, over the sea to Skye

1. Loud the winds howl, loud the waves roar, thunderclaps rend the air
Baffled our foes stand by the shore, follow they will not dare

2. Though the waves leap, soft shall ye sleep, ocean's a royal bed
Rocked in the deep, Flora will keep watch by your weary head

Skye Boat Song

3. Many's the lad fought on that day, well the claymore could wield
When the night came, silently lay dead on Culloden's field

4. Burned are our homes, exile and death scatter the loyal men
Yet, e'er the sword cool in the sheath, Charlie will come again.

Tiree Love Song

Chorus:
Hiri, hiro, my bonny wee lass, hiri, hiro, my fair one
Will you come away my love, to be my own, my rare one

1. Smiling the land, smiling the sea
Sweet was the smell of the heather,
Would we were yonder, just you and me
The two of us together.

Tiree Love Song

2. All the day long, out by the peat
Then by the shore in the gloaming
Tripping it lightly with dancing feet
And then together roaming

Weel May the Keel Row

1. Oh who is like my Johnny sae leish, sae blythe, sae bonnie
He's foremost 'mang the mony Keel lads o' coaly Tyne
He'll set or row sae tightly, or in the dance sae sprightly
He'll cut and shuffle slightly, tis true, were he not mine

Chorus:
Weel may the keel row, the keel row, the keel row
Weel may the keel row, that my laddie's in

Weel May the Keel Row

2. He has no mair o' learning, than tells his weekly earning
Yet right frae wrang discerning, though brave, nae bruiser he
Though he no worth a plack is, his ain coat on his back is,
And nane can say that black is the white o' Johnny's e'e

3. He wears a blue bonnet, blue bonnet, blue bonnet
He wears a blue bonnet, a dimple's in his chin
And weel may the keel row, the keel row, the keel row
And weel may the keel row, that my laddie's in

Wild Mountain Thyme

1. Oh the summertime is comin' and the trees are sweetly bloomin'
And the wild mountain thyme, grows around the bloomin' heather

Chorus:
Will ye go lassie go, and we'll all go together
And pick wild mountain thyme all around the bloomin' heather
Will ye go lassie go

Wild Mountain Thyme

2. I will build my love a bower by yon cool crystal fountain
And on it I'll pile all the flowers of the mountain.

3. If my true love she were gone, I would surely find another
Where the wild mountain thyme grows around the bloomin' heather

Will Ye No Come Back Again?

1. Bonnie Charlies now awa', safely o'er the friendly main
Many a heart will break in twa, should he ne'er come back again

Chorus:
Will ye no come back again? Will ye no come back again?
Better loved ye canna be, will ye no come back again?

2. Ye trusted in your Hieland men, they trusted you dear Charlie
They kent your hiding in the glen, death and exile braving.

Will Ye No Come Back Again?

3. English bribes were a' in vain, tho' puir and puirer we maun be
Siller canna buy the heart, that aye beats warm for thine and thee

4. We watched thee in the gloamin' hour, we watched thee in the mornin' grey
Tho' thirty thousand pounds they gi'e, oh, there is nane that wad betray

5. Sweet's the lav' rock's note, and lang, liltin' wildly up the glen
But aye to me he sings ae sang, "Will ye no come back again?"

Ye Jacobites By Name

Ye Jacobites By Name

LYRICS:

Flow Gently, Sweet Afton
Pages 16, 17

Flow gently, sweet Afton, among thy green braes
Flow gently, I'll sing thee a song in thy praise
My Mary's asleep by thy murmuring stream
Flow gently, sweet Afton, disturb not her dream

Thou stock dove who's echo resounds through the glen
Ye wild whistling blackbirds in yon thorny den
Thou green crested lapwing, thy screaming forbear
I charge you, disturb not my slumbering Fair

How lofty, sweet Afton, thy neighboring hills
Far marked with the courses of clear, winding rills
There daily I wander as noon rises high
My flocks and my Mary's sweet cot in my eye

How pleasant thy banks and green valleys below
Where wild in the woodlands the primroses grow
There oft as mild evening weeps over the lea
The sweet scented birk shades my Mary and me

Thy crystal stream, Afton, how lovely it glides
And winds by the cot where my Mary resides
How wanton thy waters her snowy feet lave
As gathering sweet flowerets she stems thy clear wave

Jock O' Hazeldean

Pages 22, 23

Why weep ye by the tide lady, why weep ye by the tide
I'll wed ye to my youngest son and ye shall be his bride
And ye shall be his bride, lady, so comely to be seen
But aye she let her tears down fall for Jock O' Hazeldean

Now let this willful grief be done, and dry that cheek so pale
Young Frank is chief of Errington, and Lord of Langley Dale
His step is first in peaceful ha', his sword in battle keen
But aye she let her tears down fall for Jock O' Hazeldean

A chain of gold ye shall not lack, nor braid to bind your hair
Nor mettled hound, nor managed hawk, nor palfrey fresh and fair
And you, the fairest of them all, shall ride, our forest queen
But aye she let her tears down fall for Jock O' Hazeldean

The church was decked at morning tide, the tapers glimmered fair
The priest and bridegroom wait the bride, and dame and knight were there
They sought her both in bower and ha', the lady was not seen
She's over the border and away, with Jock O' Hazeldean

Maids When You're Young

Pages 34, 35

An old man came a courtin' me, hey ding doorum down,
An old man came a courtin' me hey doorum down
An old man came a courtin' me, fain would he marry me
Maids when you're young never wed an old man

Chorus:
For he's got no falloorum faliddle faloorum
They've got no falloorum, faliddle all day
They've got no falloorum, they've lost their dingdoorum,
So maids when you're young never wed an old man

When we went to church, hey ding doorum down
When we went to church, hey doorum down
When we went to church, he left me in the lurch
Maids when you're young never wed an old man

When we went to bed, hey ding doorum down
When we went to bed, hey doorum down
When we went to bed, he lay like he was dead
Maids when you're young never wed an old man

But when he went to sleep, hey ding doorum down
But when he went to sleep, hey doorum down
But when he went to sleep, out of bed I did creep
Into the arms of a handsome young man

And he's got his faloorum faliddle faloorum
He's got his faloorum faliddle all day
He's got his faloorum and I found my dingdoorum
So maids when you're young never wed an old man